Weekly Reader Children's Book Club presents

THE FAMILY MINUS

written and illustrated by FERNANDO KRAHN

Parents' Magazine Press · New York

Copyright © 1977 by Fernando Krahn
All rights reserved. Printed in the United States of America.

Library of Congress Cataloging in Publication Data
Krahn, Fernando.
  The Family Minus.

SUMMARY: The Minus family leads an unusual life
due to some of the inventions built by Mrs. Minus.
  [1. Inventors—Fiction] I. Title.
PZ7.K8585 Fa [E]   76-18093
ISBN 0-8193-0860-9
ISBN 0-8193-0861-7 lib. bdg.

Weekly Reader Children's Book Club Edition

THE FAMILY MINUS

MR. HARRY MINUS and MRS. MARY MINUS were enjoying a deep sleep.

The alarm clock's violent ringing woke them up with a jolt.

"Exercise number two, ten times," said Mr. Minus, yawning. His wife quickly checked out an engineering problem that had kept her up last night.

Sleepy Harry Minus forgot to take off his pajama pants before jumping into the tub.

"Time to get ready for school!" Mary Minus shouted to her eight children. Then she put into action one of her favorite inventions —the automatic blanket-lifter.

To make sure they were completely awake, though, she still used a rather old-fashioned method.

Firsterix, the eldest, has never learned the right way to put his trousers on.

Fifthmore was always losing his socks, and took forever trying to find them.

Little Eightah, the only girl in the family, cried loudly every morning: "Why do I have to go to school today?"

"Hurry up!" said Mother to Secondus, Thirdly and Fourthem.
"I'm going downstairs now to get breakfast."

The breakfast call was answered with noisy enthusiasm.

Harry Minus, finished first, loved to play the flute while his children sipped their milk in rhythmic accompaniment.

With a schoolbag in one hand and an orange in the other, everybody was ready— except for Sixus who was still in the bathroom and Sevenor who forgot to put his shoes on.

"Once more, children!" shouted Father in desperation. "One, two, three, *push*!"

"Oh, I forgot to tell you, dear," said Mary Minus. "I used the car battery for my latest invention."

All eight children rushed to see what their mother had made this time. "I think," she said, "I'll be the one to take you to school today."

"I'm calling it Electrisnake Number One," she explained to her perplexed husband. "I can give you a ride to the office, too."

"Hmmm." Harry Minus pondered an instant. "I think I would rather go by bus."

To the children's delight, their mother took the most difficult— but shortest— way to school.

The school bell was ringing as Mary Minus, Firsterix, Secondus, Thirdly, Fourthem, Fifthmore, Sixus, Sevenor and Eightah made their spectacular entrance into the schoolyard.

The principal was so impressed that he cancelled classes for the first hour. A photographer was summoned to take a picture of the inventor with the entire school.

"This is just great!" exclaimed Harry Minus when he saw the photograph. And the eight little Minuses crowded around their parents. They were happy and proud to be part of the most fabulous family— Family Minus.

FERNANDO KRAHN, an accomplished picture-book artist and author, is also a successful cartoonist and filmmaker. His memorable characters are the result of a highly individualistic blend of fine draftsmanship, wit and graphic charm. Born in Chile, the artist now lives in Spain with his wife and two children. *The Family Minus* is his first book for Parents'.